Anita's Diary

MoBoni Lewis

Anita's Diary

MoBoni Lewis

Paperback Edition First Published in Great Britain in 2016 by aSys Publishing

eBook Edition First Published in Great Britain in 2016 by aSys Publishing

ISBN: 978-1-910757-73-4
aSys Publishing 2016

This book is dedicated to all the "Anita Wrights" out there.

Anita's Diary

Week One

"My application form? That'll be done tomorrow," I tell my husband, Cliff, as I hang out the washing. It's the fifth time he's asked me in the last couple of days if I've completed the form I picked up six weeks ago. He sighs resignedly and goes to bed.

* * *

Submission closes in two days, so I'm running around trying to get all the information I need. Cliff can't understand why I've left it till the last minute. I don't know why either, except that forms and I don't mix.

* * *

Application form finally completed. Hooray! Cliff drops it off for me on his way to work.

Week Two

It's Monday morning at work and everyone is alarmingly grumpy. Even the chatty ones look glum, so I keep out of their way. I make myself a cup of coffee and settle down to work when suddenly the fire alarm goes off, and we all trudge down the flight of some sixty-five stairs. But it's a false alarm, and we are soon back at our desks, but now I can't concentrate. My mind is on what I'll be having for lunch. I doodle a little bit, drawing squares and circles.

* * *

It's lunch time, and I hit the shop in earnest, buying enough food to last me for a lifetime, and soon return to work smiling like a cat that's found cream. Who ever said food doesn't make you happy?

Week Three

My youngest, Tommy, is starting big school today, so I've taken the week off work to settle him down. It's five days of half days, so I shan't be hitting the shops. There's simply not enough hours to go back and forth. I shed a few tears as I drop him off.

* * *

Back at the school to pick up my boy and he's very excited. He tells me he'd spent the day playing. I smile. Just as I'd thought.

* * *

I spent the rest of the week doing what mums do.

Week Four

My acceptance letter has arrived, and it's for the course of my choice: a six- month Psychology University Certificate. I'm thrilled. It's been a while since I had my first degree. I inform my managers at work that I'll be taking a career break. My boss is completely taken aback. He asks me if I'll be coming back. I smile mischievously. He says nothing. Then he points out that I'd just been nominated to look after the office stationary. I'm speechless. I thought we were talking about my career break! But my colleagues aren't too surprised. I think they saw it coming. We have a team meeting, and I'm asked to pass on my "wealth of knowledge" before I leave. I start emptying out my desk drawers that afternoon. I'm shocked at how much I've accumulated over the years. This place has been like my second home, but I finally get rid of all the rubbish. Seven black bin bags, not to talk of the confidential waste. Someone, please call the Litter Police!

Week Five

Taking a couple of days off to sort out some "personal stuff" in readiness for uni. It's all good.

* * *

Just spent the last few hours cooking and cleaning! Not exactly what I had in mind when I was taking time off work to sort out some "personal stuff." There's nothing personal about this, and I'm getting really upset. I've decided to go on strike just to see if my domestic prowess is appreciated or not. I never want to see another dirty dish in my life, ever again.

* * *

A day into my non-cleaning/non-hoovering strike and I'm starting to feel very uncomfortable. There are dirty dishes everywhere and there's hardly a clean cutlery in sight, but Cliff and my three boys are having the time of their life. They don't seem to have noticed that I haven't hoovered or cleaned. Unbelievable! Is it me or am I just assuming that no one really cares? Surprise, surprise—the paper plates have all disappeared, and so have the plastic cutlery.

* * *

I'm determined to make myself "heard," so I ignore the pile of dirty laundry and curl up in bed. I've hardly pulled the duvet, when my youngest, Tommy, comes running into the room, crying. He's spotted his Spiderman costume in the wash basket, which means he'll have nothing to wear for Character Day at the school tomorrow. I jump out of bed almost immediately and start chucking stuff into the washing machine, literally.

* * *

Just loaded the last wash as Cliff comes home. I try the "silent movie" approach. Surely, if I haven't said a word all evening, he'll realize how very upset I am. I'm trying so hard not to talk because I really want to.

Twenty minutes later, and I've given up. I sit Cliff down and tell him how I feel. He tells me he didn't realize I was struggling. Apparently, I've always acted like I don't need his help. And then he tells me he's been busy trying to sort out the family's finances. I feel so guilty—but even more silly—when I realize that all I needed to do was ask for help. But truth be said, I've never really been one to ask for help. Maybe it's time to shed the superwoman image for some much-needed help around the house.

Week Six

I meet the young woman who'll be replacing my position at work. Her name is Adana Brown, and we hit it off straight away. She asks me why I'm leaving and I tell her it's to pursue my dream. She's happy for me and tells me she's always wanted to be a counsellor. I tell her to follow her dream. We spend the whole day sorting out her staff details with personnel.

* * *

It's my leaving do, and I wake up feeling very nervous. I'm wondering if anyone will turn up to "send me off," but they do, and I'm surprised at the number of people who have, which makes me happy, but sad at the same time. I'm happy that people have cared enough to show up, and sad because I've always thought no one cares about me. They do the speeches and all. A lot of people are actually surprised that I have a life outside of work.

Week Seven

Cliff and I are having a "talk" about our finances since he'll be the only one working until I finish my studies. I'm waiting patiently to hear what's being axed and what isn't. The sports channels are staying, I'm told, but the movies have to go—just as I thought, but I'm not bothered. I rarely have time to watch movies, anyway.

Week Eight

First day at Uni. I look around anxiously like a kid who's just been dropped off in the middle of nowhere. Several thoughts race through my mind all at once as I watch the other students strolling around in groups. My first concern, of course, is to find the lecture rooms. I've missed my induction, so now I've got to do it all on my own. Met a couple of other students who've also missed their induction and we bond over coffee.

* * *

I'm starving, but the cafeteria is at the other end of the school. I'm reluctant to walk all the way, but a course mate encourages me to give it a try. Apparently, the food is very good, so I head over to the cafeteria in haste and, who should I see: Rick, who'd been my first-ever boyfriend. I almost pass out. We'd parted amicably, but I'd cried for days as I really liked him, but the Lord said I couldn't have him. He wasn't mine! I sit upright and try not to look in Rick's direction, but he's spotted me and comes walking up to my table, smiling. I feel like an 18- year-old again—butterflies and all—but he's not the Rick I used to know. He looks very unkempt and on his T-shirt are emblazoned words I dare not repeat. I'm shocked. He'd told me he was Christian. I thought he was. We'd gone to Bible study together. Maybe he's had a crisis of faith, I imagine. He tells me he'd dropped by to see a friend. I heave a sigh of relief. I can't imagine bumping into him every other day. And then, of course, he asks me about myself. I tell him I'm a student. He smiles and tells me he knew I would go places. Suddenly his phone rings and he has to go. I wave him off happily as he leaves. Thank God for timely interruptions.

* * *

Got home and gave Cliff a very big hug. Told him I'm glad I married him. He's chuffed, and I bet he's wondering why. Reminded God that evening, that if I ever did make a demand for something outside of his will, that he shouldn't give it to me, as though He would.

* * *

Cliff asks me this morning if I'm still glad I married him. I tell him I am, and wouldn't have it any other way. He gives me a toothy grin and a big hug. That's my man. At least now I know what floats his boat.

Week Nine

First lecture and I'm completely lost. I haven't got the slightest idea what the lecturer is on about. I ask the girl beside me, and she tells me; apparently it's not the class I'm meant to be attending. I scramble quickly out of my seat, books and all amidst stares and a few giggles, only to spend the next half an hour peering in and out of lecture rooms as I try to find my course mates. I saw one of the girls in my class some ten minutes later. She tells me an email had been sent around to inform us of a change in venue. She's surprised I hadn't got it. I smile sheepishly. I haven't checked my inbox in a week.

Week Ten

First assignment on its way. The lecturer couldn't wait to pile us up with work. But it's not like my undergraduate days. My reflexes aren't as sharp, and I'm spending twice as long trying to assimilate facts and concepts. Glad to have taken various short courses over the years; otherwise this would have been a real struggle. Should have gone back to school much earlier.

Week Eleven

The last few weeks have been really tough. Cliff and I have been arguing a lot. I know it's because of our finances. He's been feeling the pressure of the bills as they keep coming in. Told him I'll make it up to him once I started working.

* * *

One of my course mates comes to school this morning and proudly informs us that she'd been at a rave all night. Surprisingly, she looks very fresh for someone who hasn't had a good night's sleep. I smile as I remember my undergraduate days. That could easily have been me. Half an hour later, I'm dozing off—and I wasn't the one who went clubbing.

Week Twelve

We are having our family devotion when my middle son, Toby, comes up with some very startling revelation of the passage we're studying, and he's only ten. Cliff and I are completely taken aback. Neither of us have ever looked at the passage in that way. We're humbled. God can and will use anyone who makes him or herself available, even kids.

* * *

Finally getting into the flow of things at uni, and I'm not dozing off in class anymore. Praise the Lord!

Week Thirteen

My hair is in desperate need of some TLC, but I'm reluctant to ask Cliff for money. He's been doing so much lately. I let it grow out in the hope that he'll notice how frizzled it's become. Cliff always likes me looking chic, but he still hasn't noticed. I whizz around him several times, smiling, and almost put my head in his face, but he still doesn't get the hint, so I ask him as nicely as I can. He grimaces, gives me an hour long lecture on the state of our finances and then gives me the money. I thank him profusely. I don't think I've ever been so grateful in my life. The little things, we take for granted, but I'm not sure if I can keep asking Cliff for money; I'm going to have to look for something. It will, of course, have to revolve around my picking the kids from school and my lectures.

* * *

Found a few jobs but the hours aren't suitable. I almost give up when I spot an advert in a shop window for a part-time receptionist in a Dental Clinic. I'm thrilled. It's near my uni and not very far from the boys' school either. I give them a call, and they ask me to come over for an interview the following day. The owner says he likes my voice and thinks I'll make a good receptionist. I'm chuffed. I call Cliff immediately to tell him the good news. The excitement in his voice is undeniable. I remind him gently that I haven't been offered the job yet.

* * *

Just dropped the kids off at school and so now I'm going for the interview. It's for 10.00 a.m., so that gives me enough time to make a good first impression. I give my shoes a shine and smooth out the creases on my skirt. I'm determined to make myself stand out from the crowd. Arrived at the clinic with fifteen minutes to spare and soon introduce myself to the young girl at the reception desk but it's oddly quiet, except for the occasional phone calls from clients. I look around the clinic, taking in every little detail. I can already see myself behind the desk, booking appointments and flashing the clients a smile, as I'll be expected to do. A few minutes later, I'm being called in for my interview. The young girl waves me off and tells me not to worry; apparently, the boss had already told her, that he likes my voice. I smile. Talk about the favour of God. Two minutes later, however, I'm sitting in front of a vaguely familiar face. I can't remember where I have seen him before, but he seems to have recognised me and he's not smiling at all. I'm confused. Then I spot an apple on his desk, and I suddenly remember who he is; it's the guy I'd ticked off for shunting at the local supermarket a few days earlier. He said he'd had a client waiting and wanted to pay for his two very small apples quickly. I told him I was also in a hurry—and I really was—so didn't allow him to "jump the queue." How I wish I had. Anyway, he tells me smugly that the job had been taken. I'm almost in tears. I try to tell him how much I need the job, but he doesn't care. I leave feeling very sorry for myself, knowing that I could have easily gotten the job. Cliff is equally disappointed but then tells me there are lots of jobs out there. Life lesson learnt: be careful how you treat others in their time of need.

Week Fourteen

Found a job at last as a part-time Library Assistant. The pay isn't great but the hours are right. I can still drop the kids at school and attend lectures, conveniently.

* * *

Been eating a lot lately and my clothes are starting to shrink. I think it's to do with the weather. Need to watch my waistline, though, as I can't afford to buy new clothes just yet.

* * *

Got off a few bus stops earlier today and walked the rest of the journey home. Very pleased with my efforts. Rewarded myself with a huge bottle of Coke.

* * *

Nearly missed my stop today, staring at a young girl taking selfies on a crowded bus. Just couldn't take my eyes off her as she posed and pouted taking various shots and from various angles. But then she could have been a model.

Week Fifteen

Cliff is planning a family outing this weekend, to compensate the boys for being very "understanding." Our annual family holiday has been put on hold, indefinitely, so have their fortnightly trips to the cinema, but I'm really tired and would rather stay home; plus, I've got a lot of assignments to do. Cliff promises me an exciting time, so I agree to go, but only to take photographs. The boys are growing up so fast. We need to create as many memories as possible.

* * *

Picnic bag: check; sandwiches: check; drinks: check. We are ready to roll. Arrived at the park and I'm sitting comfortably ready to start taking photographs when I see a little boy wondering off while his mother busies herself on her phone. I run quickly after him before he falls off the ledge only to find the mother on my heels staring at me with hateful eyes. She snatches the young boy off me, without a word, and walks away. I bet she thought I wanted to run off with him. My boys return just in time to see what wonderful photographs I'd taken while they were on the ride. Alas, I have nothing to show them because I haven't taken any. I promise to take some amazing ones while they go on other rides.

Week Sixteen

Passing by my favourite shoe shop today. Had no intention of stopping by but the owner spots me from the shop window and tries to coax me in. Apparently, she's got some very good offers in store. I reluctantly follow her, but the moment I step inside the shop, I know I've made a huge mistake. All the shoes start calling out to me all at once. There's a particular beige and black pair with kitten heels. It's the only one left and it's in my size. The owner says I could have a 25% discount on the already reduced price, but only if I buy it today. I try the shoes on, and it's a perfect fit, but of course I can't afford it, except I put it on the card; Cliff's card. I feel a gentle nudge of the Holy Spirit not to buy the shoes, but I ignore him. I give the Lord a thousand and one reasons why I needed to. The owner brings out a few more pairs and I break into a cold sweat. She sees me sweating and asks her assistant to get me a cold drink. Suddenly, a familiar hymn begins welling up within me: "I am content with what I have, little be it or much …" I know it's God speaking to me. God has a sense of humour. I drop all the shoes and leave the shop, hurriedly. The owner is somewhat confused. It's the first time I've been in her shop without buying anything, but I've learnt that when God says "No," it's because he knows something I don't. I remember Rick. How I'd pleaded with the Lord to let me marry him, and how he'd said "No." It wasn't until some seventeen years later when I saw Rick that I knew why I'd received that answer. The shop owner calls me on my phone to find out if I was okay. I tell her I am and that I just needed to get out of her shop that very moment. I assure her it had nothing to do with her and we end the conversation. I actually feel a sense of victory.

Week Seventeen

I practically live in the library now, even though I no longer work there. I need to come out with good grades, especially now that Cliff's twenty-one- year-old niece, Adora has had a first class degree in Chemistry and has been offered a scholarship to do her postgraduate degree in one of the top universities. Adora is like my little sister and looks up to me, and I don't want to let her down, but more importantly, I don't want to let my family down. They've been very supportive, especially my Cliff.

Week Eighteen

Got told by a complete stranger today that I looked like some famous singer. Was really chuffed, until I found out who she is. I'm so trying not to be angry right now. I convince myself it's because of my new hairstyle.

Week Nineteen

Having a youth convention in church. I'm amazed at how times have changed. Can't make sense of the slang that the younger generation speak. I've always described myself as young at heart, but these kids make me feel ancient. I bet my parents felt the same. I overhear one of the other mums saying the same thing. I smile. It's good to know that I'm not alone, after all.

Week Twenty

There's just a couple of months before I finish my studies, but it feels like forever. It's probably because of the intensive nature of the course: a nine- month program compressed into six for the likes of people like me. Can't wait to finish!

Week Twenty-one

More assignments! Are you kidding me? I start counting the days before my final exams, marking off my calendar one day ahead, and it seems to be working. Cliff is concerned about my lack of sleep, but I'm just trying to make use of every opportunity I have to study.

Week Twenty-two

Taking some time off to concentrate on my coursework. I could do without having to worry about keeping a diary right now. Will be back when my exams are over.

Week Thirty-two

Exams are finally over. Thank you, Jesus. Got a new phone from Cliff to celebrate the successful completion of my course.

Week Thirty-three

Julia, Cliff's younger sister, is getting married in a couple of weeks. She's purposely waited until after my exams to tie the knot, which I think is very thoughtful, and she's asked me to be one of the aunties of the day. Julia and I have always been very close and her fiancée Tony was Cliff's school son. It really is a small world.

Week Thirty-four

Watching daytime TV with my youngest, Tommy; when an inappropriate advert pops up on the small screen. I reach for the remote control and swiftly change the channel. Tommy looks at me and calmly asks me why. Apparently, he's seen the same advert at a friend's house, many times. I gasp and then I tell him that it's "not a nice advert." He smiles, so I ask him what he thinks, and he tells me. I'm shocked. I decide there and then that it's time to have the "talk" with him. Tommy seems so much relieved afterward, but I'm wondering if I've given him too much information.

* * *

Can't get enough of my new phone now, never mind that I had to be dragged kicking and screaming into the 21st century. Just couldn't bear to part with my old brick phone. It was like parting with a dear friend. But now I'm loving my new phone, and I intend to make the most of it. Poor Cliff; I bet he's wishing he'd left me with my old phone. He hasn't said anything, but I think he prefers the 20th century me: clueless but fun. Sorry darling, but this lady is not for turning. Hey, Siri! What's for dinner?

Week Thirty-five

It's Julia's big day, and she looks really gorgeous in her flowing white wedding gown. Her bridesmaids are equally breath-taking in their matching outfits, and well-coordinated dance moves, but they are all spilling out of their dresses. A few of the men look very uncomfortable. One young girl keeps her boyfriend firmly in his seat when he tries to take a photograph of the bridal train as they dance past. I chuckle quietly to myself when I realize what's going on. I'll have to remember to speak to the brides-to-be and their maids in our church about keeping "everything in place," so as to save our men a few blushes.

Week Thirty-six

My results are here, but I'm too nervous to open the envelope, so I hand it over to Cliff, while I close my eyes. He's quiet, and my heart starts to beat really fast. Suddenly, Cliff gives me a very big hug and tells me I did extremely well. I take the envelope off him to see things for myself, and it's true. I'm very excited and start jumping up and down. My boys are also very excited, and we all hold hands and do a dance, after which we say a prayer of thanksgiving to the Lord. Somehow, the whole church has heard the news—don't ask me how. A lot of them have been very supportive, and call to congratulate me.

* * *

Attended a professional Counsellors meeting today. I feel like one of the bunch now that I've got a University certificate to go along with my various diplomas in counselling and psychology. A few of the counsellors have queried the authenticity of my qualifications just because I'd studied online, but this should keep them quiet. Sadly, they aren't in the meeting today. The others welcome me with open arms like they've always done. I'm all smiles. Will be displaying my certificate proudly on my office wall.

Week Thirty-seven

I'm starting my work placement with Sharon Biggle, tomorrow. Sharon and I have worked together in the Counselling Department in church for years and get on really well, but I'm wondering what it'll be like working with her outside church.

* * *

Sharon is really good at what she does. She tells me that she loves to help people and I can see that in the way she talks to her clients. I've been counselling people for a decade, and haven't seen the level of attention that Sharon gives to her clients, even though many of them aren't Christians. I've got a lot to learn from this lovely woman of God.

* * *

Sharon gives me a side room for my "clients." I'm very excited and set about putting my personal touches on my own little room. This really is a dream come true.

* * *

The boys come round to "see" mummy's new office, but they aren't impressed. My five year old thinks it's not "cool." I ask him to give me a couple of months for me to make it the coolest office in town, but he's not convinced. Cliff takes us all out to celebrate my new office.

Week Thirty-eight

Got an email from my best friend, Dora Page, asking me to come over for a few days. I'm excited, and I jump at the opportunity to be waited on hand and foot. Sharon has given me a couple of days off as the kids are on holiday, so I'll be "jetting off" to Dora's. But Cliff isn't too keen on me going. He's worried how he'll cope with the boys while I'm away. I write him a "booklet" of things to do. He's taken aback and asks me to consider taking the youngest with me. I laugh till my belly starts to hurt. I then write him a one-page version of the "booklet." He's happy and soon sends me off with his blessings.

Anita's Diary

* * *

On the way to Dora's and wondering what our meeting will be like. Dora and I have been best of friends since primary school. She's the only one who's been there for me, but I'm worried about our friendship now. Dora is still trusting God for a child after ten years of marriage, and here I am with three lovely boys. I'd have to remember not to gush about my kids as I often do. Perhaps we could talk about my work placement. I suddenly realize that there's really not a lot we can talk about, but I'm hoping for a lovely time, all the same. We are no longer the eighteen-year-olds we used to be, talking about guys all night long. We're both grown women now and married to men who'd crossed the ocean, literally to be with us. Lord, please give me wisdom.

* * *

Huge house, four cars, and a massive indoor swimming pool; Dora is living the life, and she even has someone waiting on her every need. Wow!

* * *

Just two days at Dora's and I can't wait to go back home. I've been given almost everything that money can buy, but I'm desperate for human company, Dora's in particular. After all, she invited me over. I love Dora, but she's far too busy, plus she and her husband George are in their own world.

* * *

Got talking to Dora's chef today. His name is Kande, and he has two degrees in English. No wonder he speaks like the Queen or King, whichever one it is. Complimented him on his cooking and that he'll soon be a household name. His

19

meals are actually very tasty.

* * *

Went to Church with Dora today. Massive, massive church, with people from so many different nationalities. Enjoyed the sermon and everyone seemed genuinely happy. Couldn't help but wonder if they all had huge houses like Dora.

* * *

Sunday lunch with the Pages's and there's so much variety. Kande has spent all morning cooking. I ask Dora if we were having guests, but she says "No." It is all for me. I smile, but I'm starting to wonder if Dora is more interested in showing off than she is in spending time with me. The food is really nice, but George has to go out to meet some business partner, so his meal was untouched. Kande seems very upset, and I can understand why. I would if I'd spent the whole morning preparing three different dishes for three people.

* * *

Got a call from Cliff and I can hear the boys howling in the background. They seem to be having so much fun. One of them shouts a hurried "hello," but won't come to the phone. I'm completely taken aback. I thought they would have been asking me to come back home, but it appears they aren't missing me at all. Have a little pity party feeling sorry for me.

* * *

It's the day before I return home. Dora and I finally get a chance to talk, and she tells me that she and George are actually on the brink of a divorce, which of course, was why they'd been trying so hard to put on a united front. And they are about to lose the house, too. George's business isn't doing very well, and they are in so much debt. She says she wanted me to come over before the house is repossessed. And they are still believing in God for a child. I hug Dora and tell her everything is going to be okay. I pray with her and tell her God would come through for them.

* * *

Kande is sad to see me leave. He says I've been such an inspiration over the recent days. Asks me if I would come to his wedding the following year. I tell him I couldn't promise but that I would try to make an appearance, provided I am given enough notice.

* * *

Back home and everyone is surprisingly glad to have me back, but for one reason: They've missed my cooking. But the house is in a mess, so I start barking orders right from the front door. The boys start picking up their stuff, almost immediately. Cliff lets me finish the "marching order," then gives me a big hug and tells me he's missed me. I notice that he's put on some weight. They must have had fries, four days in a row.

* * *

Week Thirty-nine

The second week in my new office and a young couple have come for pre-marital counselling. Sharon is off for a couple of weeks, so it's up to me to attend to the clients. I'm nervous and excited at the same time. I ask the Lord for wisdom and put on my best professional voice, asking the young couple how they'd met. They both seem genuinely in love with each other. It reminds me of when Cliff and I were courting. "So what exactly do you see in each other?" I ask. The young man looks lovingly at his fiancée and tells me that she has the most beautiful smile he's ever seen. "And he has a very good sense of humour," the girl returns. I smile nervously. I look at the two love birds as they go on and on about their hopes and aspirations for the future. There's even a name-dropping session where I get to know who they hang out with, but there's no mention of God in all their conversation, so I ask if they are Christians. "Oh yeah!" the young man replies enthusiastically. Apparently, they've both been baptized as young kids. I know at that point that they aren't saved, so ask them if they'd like to meet the only one who can knit their hearts together in love. Both seem puzzled but keen. I give them the gospel as simply as I can, and both give their hearts to the Lord. Praise the Lord! I refund their counselling fees as my gift towards their forthcoming nuptials.

* * *

Arrived home to find the house looking spotless. Cliff has done the hoovering, and he's cooked me dinner, too. I feel very loved. I give him a big hug. The kids hear my voice and come running down the stairs, but I send them back to their rooms. Cliff and I spend some much needed time together, but he soon falls asleep while I'm talking.

Week Forty

No two days are alike, which is one reason why I love what I do; but today's couple has got me thinking really hard. The husband's threatening to leave the wife because, according to him, she's now three times the size she was when they got married and, in his own words, he doesn't do fat. The poor woman has tried every diet but is unable to shift the weight after having three wonderful kids.

I sit there looking at her while the husband sits a few metres away. He can't even bear to look at his own wife. I glance briefly at our wedding photo on my desk. I am no longer the svelte size twelve I was when Cliff and I got married, and I briefly thank God for the fact that Cliff hadn't fallen in love with me for my figure. Nonetheless, I make up my mind to register at the gym as soon as possible. I look in the husband's direction and notice that he has a beer belly, and I ask them both to try power walking in the evenings. The husband gives me an evil look. I think he feels insulted.

* * *

Got home and did a twirl as Cliff watched footie. I ask him what he thinks about my weight. He smiles, without even looking in my direction, so I leave the room, somewhat convinced that he doesn't really mind.

* * *

Doing the weekly shopping with Cliff when I spot some chocolate bars on offer. I buy a few and drop them in the trolley. Cliff looks alarmed. He tells me I need to watch my calorie intake. Apparently, my dresses are starting to look a little tighter around the waist. I glare at him and return the chocolate bars, but one.

* * *

At the gym to register today. Got all the leaflets and the healthy eating plan. I feel empowered. I might even try the shakes for lunch.

Week Forty-one

It's party season, and this time, it's a thirty-seventh birthday party. A friend of Cliff's has turned thirty-seven and has invited us round. But it's almost the same crowd as the one we attended a couple of weeks ago, so I can't wear the same dress, plus it's going to be on Facebook. Don't want to be tagged as the lady who keeps wearing the same outfit at every gathering. I once got asked by a little girl some years ago, if I only had one pair of shoes, after having been caught wearing the same pair on two different occasions. But Cliff isn't bothered. I love his outlook on life. The party is fun but finishes late. I get back home just before midnight.

* * *

Sunday service. I can barely keep my eyes open. One of my Sunday School kids asks me if I'd partied all night. Cheeky! Will be knocking off early tonight.

Week Forty-two

I'm really enjoying my work placement; plus, Sharon has asked me to stay on to work with her. Wish I'd done this years ago. Cliff's been working from home a lot, so he's been dropping the kids off at school and picking them up. I think he's starting to appreciate how much I had to do in the early years.

Anita's Diary

* * *

It's Cliff's birthday in a few days, and I've got a surprise for him, but I'm not sure how I'm going to pull it off, without him knowing since he now knows most of my contacts. We'll see.

* * *

Got a call from an old school mate, Desiree Shinnay. She's in town and wants to meet up. I'm completely taken aback. Desiree and I weren't the best of friends in school, but she seemed really excited when we spoke on the phone, so I've decided to meet up with her. But Cliff isn't too keen on me meeting with Desiree. Desiree doesn't think much of him, plus we're having to rearrange our whole lives to accommodate her request. But I assure Cliff it'll be worth it in the end. Desiree is probably wanting to apologize for the way she'd bullied me all through school, so why deny her the opportunity to "right" her "wrongs." I make a list of the times Desiree's upset me so that we can "talk things through." She probably doesn't realize how much she'd hurt me. I'm shocked at how much I can still remember after all these years.

* * *

Meeting Desiree for lunch today, and surprisingly I'm starting to feel like the unpopular sixteen-year-old girl I was nearly two decades ago. I'm really not liking this. I'm tempted to call off our lunch, but Desiree has already messaged me to say that she's in the neighbourhood. Lord, please help me get through this.

* * *

Half an hour later, Desiree and I are having lunch, and she hasn't changed a bit. She tells me I've put on a lot of weight.

I smile, but deep down I really want to smack her. Why does she have to point that out and then go on and on about everything and everyone? I hardly get a chance to put in a word. She stops to take a glass of water, and I quickly start talking. Just then Desiree's husband, Ray calls, and Desiree has to go. I stare in disbelief as she says a quick goodbye without having touched her food. I'm still sulking when the waiter brings the bill, and its' much more than I've budgeted for. I reluctantly pay the bill, ignoring the tip. Part of me is tempted to ask for Desiree's meal to be packed up in a takeaway bag, but I resist the temptation and quietly leave the restaurant.

* * *

I return home and burst into tears as soon as I walk through the front door. Cliff holds me and lets me cry for as long I want. He doesn't even ask me why I am crying, but I think he has guessed. Desiree has been a huge part of our lives. Her negative comments have plagued me for years, so much so that I once thought no one would want to be with me, even Cliff. It took me several years of telling myself that I was beautifully and wonderfully made, to get me out of the rut. My youngest, Tommy is shell-shocked when he sees me crying and soon returns with his teddy, which he plonks on my lap. It's his "make me feel better Teddy." I smile and hug him. Surprisingly, I feel much better. I tell myself that the next time I see Desiree, she'll be having it from me! That's if I ever get to see her again.

* * *

Got to the gym today, but was too scared to go in. I see all the young people with their gadgets "marching" in. Many of them don't look like they need to be here, but, of course, we all have different reasons for going to the gym. I'm waiting in my car when I spot one of the mums whose son share's the same class as my eldest son, Tony. She's about my size and she's walking confidently to the gym in her Lycra. I'm shocked. I couldn't possibly do that, but she's strutting away. I quickly open the car door and call out to her, and we both make our way to the gym. She tells me she comes here four times a week. I tell her it's my first time. We start working out, or rather "talking out," but it's a start.

* * *

Woke up this morning and could hardly get out of bed. I'm aching all over from yesterday's workout. Cliff tells me it'll get better with time. Thankfully, it's a Saturday, so there's no rush to get the kids to school. I put an old picture of me in my purse to spur me on.

Week Forty-three

It's Cliff's birthday. I've booked a table at our favourite restaurant. He thinks we're just going out for a meal, but I've invited a couple of our close friends. Cliff has been a wonderful husband and father, and I just want him to know how much I love and appreciate him.

We head out for the evening, holding hands. The restauranteur, Madge, is also in on the surprise and soon puts on a happy birthday song as soon as Cliff and I walk in. I pretend to be surprised as Cliff looks around the beautifully decorated dining space. Madge is a personal friend and had put in some finishing touches. I'm loving the look of surprise on Cliff's face. Then our friends begin to arrive. First was Matt and Abi, followed by Grace and Adam, and then Bill and Kezia. Cliff's mouth drops as he suddenly realizes what's going on. It's a wonderful evening. Cliff is more relaxed than I've seen him in a very long time, and he tells me he's enjoying himself—and that he loves me! Job done!

Week Forty-four

Been feeling very tired lately, so I've have stopped going to the gym. Cliff suggests I see the doctor. I don't really want to, but he's already booked me in, so, I might as well.

* * *

Sitting at the doctors and feeling very nervous, but the doctor has a huge smile on her face as she returns to the office. I've just had a urine test. She tells me I'm nearly five months pregnant. I almost fall off my chair. Apparently, my baby has been "hiding." I'm somewhat numb. How could I have missed that? With my three boys, I knew within weeks that I was pregnant. She tells me every pregnancy is different, and slightly infers that my weight could have played a part in concealing the bulge. I ignore the latter, but I know she doesn't mean any harm. And then I remember that my cycle hasn't been regular for months, making it almost impossible to keep an accurate record of "anything," really. Doctor hands me a few leaflets and prescribes some folic acid. She also books me in for a scan. I leave the doctors, completely dazed.

* * *

Cliff isn't home when I return. He's taken the boys out for a pizza. That gives me enough time to process things, but once I do, I'm all excited. Not sure what Cliff is going to make of this, though. We've already given out all baby-related items in our household. At first, Cliff thinks I'm telling a fib, but the look on his face is priceless when he realizes it's true. Let's pray it's a girl; he tells me, excitedly. After three very energetic boys, I can understand why he wants a girl. I'm not so fussed. I'll gladly take whatever God gives us, but a girl will be nice, and if it is, I hope she'll take after my love for anything vintage. At least then, I wouldn't have to throw or give away my treasured collection. But that's still a long time to come, anyway.

Week Forty-Five

It's morning sickness like I've never had in my life. It's funny, though, considering that I wasn't even feeling nauseous before I went to the doctors. I convince myself it's just in my head, but after camping in the loo, I realize that it's not in my head. Cliff buys me a puke bag.

* * *

Can't keep anything down and have suddenly developed a craving for ice cream—Ben and Jerry's. Can't count the number of calories I've wolfed down in the last few days. Cliff is starting to get worried, but more for his wallet. Those ice creams don't come cheap.

* * *

Spent the whole day being waited on hand and foot. I'm loving it. I could get used to this.

Week Forty-six

I overhear the boys saying they'd like a little sister and what they'd call her. How sweet. Cliff and I haven't even thought of a name yet. The morning sickness is starting to subside, thankfully, and the cravings have stopped. Cliff is doubly excited. He tells me he's glad to have his wife back. Aawww!

* * *

It's Mother's day. Got the most beautiful card from my boys. Didn't know when I started to cry. It's times like this that we realize what impressions we make on our kids. My little man, Tommy offers to stay with me till I "feel better." Bless!

Week Forty-seven

We're going for our first scan, and I'm very nervous. What if it's not a girl? Cliff will be very disappointed, and so will the boys. I would be, too, I think. We've all been looking forward to having another girl in the house.

And it's a girl! Cliff rubs his hands in glee. I've never seen him so excited. The boys jump around excitedly when we tell them, and then the names start coming: Chloe, Anastasia, Gabrielle, even Pinky. I couldn't stop laughing. We might have to pull a name out of a hat at this rate.

Week Forty-eight

Cliff is starting work on the nursery this week. It's been three years since we turned the third bedroom into a "box" room, literally, so he is having to turn it back into a bedroom. His best mate, Andy has offered to give him a hand, so hopefully, we should have the nursery ready in a couple of weeks. My boys are super excited and offer to help too. Anything for their little sister.

* * *

Feel like ripping out the newly laid carpet in the nursery. The smell is making feel nauseous. Cliff advises me to stay away, but I want to see what they're doing. Don't want any surprises after it's finished, but Tony assures me that everything will be fine. Will have to trust the boys on this one.

* * *

My oldest two are having a "talent contest, " and they've asked me to be the judge. This is going to be very tricky as both are very talented but at different things. Tony is very athletic, and Toby loves his books; he'll read anything in print and has a knack with words. Tony is 11 and Toby is 10. Half an hour later and the little one is asking to join in. I couldn't stop laughing. He's only just turned five. This is going to be fun. I've devised a way to help me judge fairly. Everyone will sing the same song; we'll record it and then play it over.

* * *

My boys sing their hearts out, each getting a standing ovation from bump and me, and after ten minutes I'm giving them my verdict. I've never seen my boys being so competitive. It is so scary.

I tell them that having carefully listened to the recordings; I think they'll make a good boy band. I say they each have something unique. Everyone seems happy. It's going much better than I'd thought. I settle down to eat my prawn sandwich.

Week Forty-nine

Woke up to the sight of a very excited Tony who tells me that since last week's evaluation of their talent contest, he and his brothers have decided to form a boy band, and they are already looking for a label to sign them on. Oh no, what have I done? I scramble out of bed almost immediately and try to explain what I meant, but it falls on deaf ears. My little one asks me why I won't let them sing if they were really good. I ask the boys about their education and get a cheeky smile in return. The members of the most prolific boy band, I'm told, never had a formal education. The boys have surely done their homework. Spend the next half an hour trying to talk my boys out of their "dream," but they are adamant. Lord, I need your help.

* * *

Cliff is back from playing golf with his mates, and I quickly tell him about what the boys have decided, then waddle back to bed. Two hours later, the boys come into our room. They've struck a deal with Cliff, Tony tells me. If they all get straight A's all year round, then a boy-band could be on the cards. Nice try Cliff, but I hope you're ready.

Week Fifty

Got a text from Dora. Kande's wedding is in four weeks, and he wants me to attend. I start to feel very uncomfortable. As much as I want to be a part of Kande's big day, a part of me is reluctant to attend simply because of Dora. I'm not sure how she'll react to my unexpected blessing, knowing that she's still believing in God for a child. And there's no hiding. I'll be huge by then. I ask God to please give Dora a child, too. She has so much love to give.

Week Fifty-one

My doctor asks me to take things easy, so I'm taking some time off work, doing nothing. But, I can't get Dora off my mind. I'll make a few calls to reschedule some counselling appointments.

* * *

The boys have been coming home from school with tons of homework, and I'm beginning to wonder if their teachers are just piling them up with work instead of teaching them in class. My oldest two are getting really stressed, plus we haven't received feedback on their work. Cliff will be having a word with the school tomorrow.

* * *

Cliff was at the boys' school today. It turns out that the head-teacher is trying to impress the school governors by claiming to have covered the school syllabus in record time. Very interesting—and at the expense of our kids.

Week Fifty-two

I don't do social media, but the swimming club that Tony attends has decided to embrace Facebook as their main channel of communication with their clients, so I'm now on it. Got a number of friend requests in the first week and accept them all, without a second glance. If I'm going to be on it, I might as well as go large.

* * *

Got a few more friend requests today and accept them all, yet again. Haven't got a clue who they are, but hey, who cares. The more, the merrier. Feeling very popular right now.

* * *

I'm being bombarded with messages every day. Can't keep up! I decide to opt out for a couple of days.

* * *

Arrived at the Swimming Club today to be told that lessons for the week have been cancelled for health and safety reasons, and it's been posted on Facebook. Now how exactly did I miss that?

Week Fifty-three

Cliff and I are going clothes shopping. I've got nothing to wear for Kande's wedding. I may be pregnant, but I plan to turn up looking stylish, nonetheless. Cliff finds me a nice burgundy evening gown.

* * *

Dora calls me to find out if we're still coming. I tell her we are. She seems really excited, and I'm wondering if things are back to normal with her and George. She hasn't said anything about him, but I'm reluctant to ask. The last time I did she'd cried for over an hour, but I hope they stay together. They are a great couple.

Week Fifty-four

It's Kande's big day. The kids have all been shipped off to Julia for the weekend, so Cliff and I have the day to ourselves. I tell him how I feel about meeting Dora and he assures me all will be well. Dora and I have come a long way, he tells me, and she's sure to be very happy for me.

* * *

The car pulls up at Kande's wedding when baby decides to give me a kick. How appropriate. I wince in pain. Just then, Dora makes an appearance wearing a white, floaty gown, with George by her side, and she's smiling. Then I notice a bulge from under her gown, and I almost scream with delight. Dora is pregnant, which means I don't have to hide anymore. I get out of the car, holding on to Cliff. Dora looks at me and then at Cliff as if to say "what happened?" I'd told her we were done with having kids. Cliff shrugs his shoulders, smiling. In that moment, Dora whispers into my ears. She and George are expecting twin girls, and she's nearly eight months pregnant.

"Praise the Lord!" I scream, looking Dora over. I ask her why I had been kept in the dark. She tells me she didn't want to spoil the surprise, but I wish she had. All those months I'd spent wondering how I was going to share my "good news" with her.

* * *

Kande's wedding was brilliant, and his wife looked amazing. Popped over to wish them a happy married life with a small gift and then we were off to Dora's. Dora and I spent the evening comparing notes. I find out we'd gotten pregnant about the same time, without knowing. Hope our kids are just as close.

Week Fifty-five

Our eldest, Tony is off to secondary school in a couple of days. How time flies. I pop over to his room to give him some last minute briefings, and he's on his bed, wearing a hoodie with the hood on. I'm not a huge fan of hoodies, but I don't want to be distracted from my mission, so I let him be. I've already spoken to him a few times about not wearing his hood indoors. Don't really see why he should, but he seems to enjoy "hiding" as it were. Anyway, I give him an hour long lecture on secondary school life. He thinks I'm being overly protective, but I drum it in, all the same. He's a little bit quiet, but I'm sure he's listening. Then I ask him if he has any questions, but I don't get any reply. I take his hood off and see that my boy has fallen fast asleep. I'm shocked. Don't know exactly how long he's been asleep for, but I'm hoping that he's heard most of what I had to say.

* * *

My middle son, Toby has come back from school and is exceptionally quiet. I'm convinced it's because he misses his big brother who is now in secondary school. They've always done everything together. I try to tease him, but it's not working. After ten minutes of prodding and talking, he finally tells me he's fallen out with his best mate, Mark over some girl called Ruby. Apparently, Mark now likes Ruby and doesn't want to hang out with my boy anymore, and they've been friends since kindergarten. I can't believe it; Mark is only ten. Anyway, I pull Toby close and tell him not to worry and things would eventually sort themselves out. He nods and wipes his tears. I kind of feel sorry for him. Kids have feelings too, and sometimes we forget that.

Week Fifty-six

Feeling a lot stronger, so I've decided to go back to work for a few weeks before I go on maternity leave. Many of my clients are glad to have me back, but this time I'm taking things easy. I realize that I've actually missed coming to work.

* * *

Toby and Mark are friends again! Ruby has decided that she doesn't like Mark after all. Girls—they grow up quick!

* * *

Tony has returned home from the shops, seemingly upset. I'm worried he's been involved in a fight, but he tells me he was picked on by a security guard for wearing his hood on the shop floor in one of the stores. I point out gently that most shops have a "no hood policy" for security reasons. He sees my point and immediately apologizes for having flouted my instructions about not wearing his hood indoors. I smile gently and draw him close. It's not very often that my Tony admits to being wrong. I'm trying so very hard not be smug right now.

Week Fifty-seven

Sharon is thinking of moving to another office. She thinks I have what it takes to run the practice on my own. Apparently, many of her clients are very happy with the level of care and attention I give to them, and she's happy for me to take them on. I'm shocked. This woman is unbelievable! Who would hand over her clients to someone else, just like that? I thank

Sharon profusely for the trust she has in me and promise not to let her down. I put an advert out almost immediately, letting out Sharon's office.

* * *

Had a pretty young professional stop by the practice today, wanting to hire Sharon's office. She's a family lawyer, specializing in divorces, and wondered if she could move in when Sharon moves out. She tells me she's very good at what she does, and I have no doubts about that, but I politely decline. It just didn't feel right having a divorce lawyer in the very office where we're trying to counsel people to save their marriage.

Week Fifty-eight

Got the invoice for the practice today and it's for the same amount that the young lady was willing to pay for hiring Sharon's room for her legal practice. Now having second thoughts. Maybe I should I have given her the benefit of the doubt; after all, she's only doing her job.

Week Fifty-nine

It's my last week in the office. Gave myself a send-off with chicken ribs.

Week Sixty

Doing some more baby shopping. The thing about having a girl is that there are so many pretty things on offer. I'm reminding myself to go easy. Kids grow up so quickly.

Week Sixty-one

Having a barbecue when my waters break. Cliff springs into action almost immediately. Thankfully, it's a Saturday, and we've got friends round. We hand over the boys to Bill and Kezia and rush to the hospital. Destiny arrives almost immediately, and she's the most beautiful baby ever. Cliff is over the moon and soon begins posting on social media about his newest arrival.

* * *

Return home to three excited boys. This little girl in very good hands.

Week Sixty-two

It's Destiny's Christening and all our friends have gathered at ours after the church service. My youngest, Tommy, seems to have grown up all of a sudden as he helps to serve the drinks. I think he's finally realised that he's no longer the baby of the house. Everyone is excited as they help themselves to copious amounts of food and drinks.

* * *

The party is over, and everyone is heading home when George's call comes through. Dora has also given birth. I send her a quick congratulatory message with a photo of Destiny in her christening gown. I'm really so very happy for Dora.

Week Sixty-three

Destiny and I are just getting into a routine when Cliff comes home from work to say he's being posted abroad to head a project. I almost drop Destiny's bottle in shock, but he tells me to look on the bright side of things. He'll soon be back, and we'll have more funds at our disposal. I reluctantly agree, but the thought of not having to count the pennies did make me feel less grumpy.

Week Sixty-four

Cliff is off in a couple of days, and I'm helping him pack his bags, but I soon have a total meltdown. My boys are shocked. They'd never seen me cry this much, so Cliff takes them aside and makes them all promise to look after me while he's gone.

Week Sixty-five

It's Cliff's first week away, and the boys, and I are struggling to get into a routine, with Destiny. I'm thinking of getting some help.

* * *

Found a couple of young girls on gap year looking to make some extra bucks in the local paper. Hopefully, one of them will be willing to help me around the house and with the boys until Cliff comes back.

* * *

Anita's Diary

The first appointment is this afternoon. It's a foreign student called Stompey and her resume is very impressive. I show the boys Stompey's photograph for them to tell me what they think; after all, she'll be looking after them. My youngest, Tommy, pulls a face. He says Stompey hasn't got a smiling face. I explain to him that it's a passport photograph, and people are not expected to smile, but he's still not happy and walks off, quietly.

* * *

Stompey turns up for the appointment and doesn't have a smiling face, still. I'm slightly worried. The boys say "Hello!", but she just stares. I'm starting to think that Tommy was right after all. I was just about to tell Stompey how impressive her resume was when she tells me she's allergic to most cleaning products, including washing-up liquid, and she doesn't do school pick-ups and drop-offs. I then ask her what she'll be doing, and all I get is a stony stare. The boys aren't impressed. I thank Stompey for her time and tell her I won't be employing her. She seems quite relieved and waltzes out of my house with a smile on her face, and then promptly ticks me off the list she's holding. I'm puzzled. Was this a box-ticking exercise or did she really need a job, but then she sounded really desperate when I spoke to her over the phone. Or was it someone else?

* * *

Five interviews and all of the girls want to work on their own terms. I feel helpless and call Cliff to ask him if he's able to come back earlier than planned. The answer, of course, is "No!" so I tell the boys we'll be working with military precision from now on. I draw a chart and tell everyone what they have to do and when, and there are gold stars and pressies to be won.

* * *

First day of our new regime. Tony is up early and helps get Tommy ready for school, freeing me up to feed Destiny. He seems to be stepping up to the challenge. I'm seeing a very different Tony.

Week Sixty-six

We're operating like newly oiled pieces of equipment. Everything is going smoothly. This can only be God, and the boys are enjoying their newly found independence. They are actually capable of doing a lot more than I'd thought. Like Cliff, they've simply allowed me to get on with things, all because I didn't get them involved. This is an eye-opener. Got to tell Cliff this.

* * *

It's half term next week, and I'm slightly worried about keeping the boys occupied. We've lost our internet connection, so were pretty much in the dark ages. And the nearest theme park is several miles away. I'll have to come up with something very creative for the kids to do for next week. I ask Cliff to speak to his best mate, Andy to see what can be done about our internet connection.

Week Sixty-seven

First day of half term and my boys are already bored, plus it's been raining all day, so playing in the garden has been ruled out. I come up with a game of "I spy," but after two sessions they've had enough, so I bring out a Monopoly board, but there's no dice. Tommy suggests using his pencil rubber as dice. It's a rubber in the shape of a dice, and it works perfectly. We do a few rounds and *ta-da!* it's dinner time. One down, four to go. I stay awake all night, wondering what to do with my troop tomorrow.

* * *

My friend, Esther rings me up. She's got extra football tickets and would like to take my kids to watch a match at the stadium, with her son. I want to hug her. The boys are super excited and spend the whole day talking about their favourite team. Thankfully, they all support the same team, so there won't be any arguments should the other team win. Nearly there!

* * *

Just me and Destiny at home today, and we spend the whole day catching up on sleep!

* * *

It's day four of half term, and it's going to be Arts and Crafts Day. Tony isn't keen on drawing, but Toby and Tommy make a go of it—for about an hour or two, and then the sun comes out, and they all run outside for a game of footie for the rest of the day.

* * *

Last day of half term and I've decided to take the boys to the cinema, but they can't decide on what to watch, so I end up having to choose. It's a family movie, with a great message and the boys love it. I get back home and begin getting their uniform ready for school. Can't believe we survived a whole week without Wi-Fi.

* * *

Andy has managed to fix our internet connection. Just time in time for Father's day! We skype Cliff to wish him a Happy Father's Day.

* * *

Taking a break from writing. Will be doing a video diary until Cliff comes home. Want him to see his daughter's every minute.

Week Eighty-four

Time flies. Cliff is back next week after being away for five months, so I've resumed writing. I've got some awesome clips of Destiny for him, and of the boys, too. I'm sure he'll love them.

Week Eighty-five

Cliff is back. The boys jump all over him, excitedly. Destiny turns around the moment she hears his voice. Cliff picks her up and won't put her down. She was just a week old when Cliff was posted abroad. Destiny soon falls asleep in her father's arms.

* * *

It's 9.00 p.m., and Cliff is wondering why Tommy hasn't called for him. He normally runs a bath for the little one before he goes to bed. So he goes round to check and finds the boys fast asleep. He's shocked and comes running downstairs. He thinks the boys have flunked their nightly routine. I tell him his sons have learned to sort themselves out. As he settles down to watch footie, he smiles and then tells me that he might be going away more often.

* * *

Destiny's keeping me busy. She doesn't compromise her night feeds at all. I'm on autopilot, most of the time, but I wouldn't change this for anything. She's such a blessing. Thank you, Lord.

* * *

Thinking of going back to work very soon. I'm going to miss staying home with Destiny, but I do love my job and would like to go back.

Week Eighty-six

Checking out Destiny's nursery today. It's the same one Tommy had attended, but that was years ago. Need to make sure that the nursery's standards are still the same. Everything looks scarily the same at first glance, which I thought was weird, and now Cliff has decided to park in the same bay we used to park in when dropping Tommy off. I feel slightly dizzy and hold on to Cliff. It's like going backward in time. The proprietor seems extremely surprised to see me. She says she wasn't aware that I'd been pregnant. I smile, but she's looking at me funny, and also at Destiny. Not sure what she's thinking, but I'm not having someone stare at my daughter like that, so I point out, nicely, that Destiny's got her father's eyes and my nose. She takes a second and closer look and then smiles at me, but she still hasn't told me what she was looking for. She later tells us that they've had a recent case of child abduction and now all parents have to be questioned. I nod, politely, but I think she could have been more tactical. What if Destiny had been adopted? Cliff isn't too impressed, but I quickly nudge him before he kicks off. This is the only nursery in our area that's willing to cater for children less than a year old.

* * *

Dropping Destiny off at Nursery today but she's holding on to my top, so tightly and won't let go. I tell the proprietor that it appears Destiny isn't ready yet. We'll be back tomorrow.

* * *

Back at the nursery again and Destiny is holding on tight, yet again. I drop her off anyway, but my heart isn't at peace. A couple of hours later, I'm back at the nursery, only to find the nursery door ajar and Destiny wet to her skin. Her diaper hasn't been changed, and her bib is so dirty I can't even look at it. The proprietor is on the phone in her office chatting away and seems very surprised to see me. She asks me how I got in, and I tell her the door was ajar. She says I should have knocked all the same, for health and safety reasons. I don't argue with her, but simply point out that Destiny won't be returning to the nursery. She tells me I won't be getting a refund. I tell her she can keep it; my baby's life is more important. Was just about to leave when she pulls me back and asks me not to tell the authorities. Apparently, this was a one-off case. She then offers to take me around the nursery; she shows me the other children in their playpens; more like cages, if you ask me. There is hardly a smiling face in sight. My heart breaks for the kids. One of them puts her hands out to be carried, but I'm told I can't. I leave the nursery almost in tears, as Destiny puts her head on my bosom. This was the same nursery my youngest son attended and which was very much in demand back then. I had to register Tommy the week after I found out I was pregnant in order to secure a place for him. It was that competitive. Don't know what's happened to this place, but whatever it is, it's not looking good.

* * *

Cliff is surprised to see Destiny at home. I tell him why I'd gone back to pick her. He tells me he's felt the same way when I was dropping her off but didn't want to stand in the way of my going back to work. I feel a sense of guilt and ask the Lord to forgive me for overriding my conscience, especially when there's no urgent need for me to go to back to work just yet. I do miss my work, no doubt, but Destiny needs me now. I'm sure my clients would understand.

Week Eighty-seven

Got a hamper from one of my clients today, just to say "Thank you," with a photograph, but I can't tell who they are. I take a closer look at the photograph, and it's the couple who I'd once counselled; the ones who were about to go their separate ways because the husband thought his wife had put on too much weight. I'm in awe. The woman looks twenty years younger, and the man has lost his beer belly, and both look really happy. In the hamper is a card, thanking me for encouraging them to power-walk together. I can't stop smiling. This is why I love my job. It really is rewarding.

Week Eighty-eight

I'm actually enjoying staying at home, now. I'm able to help the kids with their homework a lot more, and we've established an even closer bond. Tommy looks forward to lunch now, knowing that it's not leftover food from the night before. I really am grateful to God for the opportunity to stay home and for Cliff's job otherwise, this wouldn't have been possible. I write a "Thank you" note to Cliff for being such a hardworking husband and father.

Week Eighty-nine

The young mums at Tommy's school have recently upped their game, turning up at the school gate with a full face at 8.30 a.m.—and I mean a full face. My tracksuit buddies have also joined in, and now Tommy won't allow me to leave the house if I don't "dress up." I try to tell him that mummy has been up all night, feeding his little sister and just wants to drop them off in school and go back to bed, but he's not taking "No" for an answer, so I'm going to have to sacrifice a few winks to dress up for my boy.

* * *

Got dressed today and had some makeup on. Tommy is really happy. He tells me I look *really* nice. I hug my little man but tell him I can't promise him I'll look like this every day. Cliff comes home from work to see me all dressed up and points out subtly that he'd like to see me all dolled up more often. I tell him most of my clothes don't fit anymore. He nods and walks away smiling.

* * *

I'm starting to enjoy dressing up again, and I always look forward to it, even if it's just for the school run. But I'm not going for a full face, not when I have to go back to bed afterward.

* * *

One of the mums complimented me on my appearance today. I feel like an entirely new person. Return home from the school run to find a parcel waiting. Cliff has ordered some new clothes for me, and they are really beautiful. I'm really going to have to make an effort now.

Week Ninety

Went shopping today and saw some really nice Christmas cards on display. I love Christmas, but Cliff, and I have decided to do things differently this time around. We'll be donating toys to a Children's Charity instead of buying multiple toys for the children; the boys will still get to choose a present each. They need to know that Christmas is more about giving than receiving.

* * *

The boys are busy preparing for the Nativity play in church. Everyone's bagged a part this year, so there's a lot of rehearsals going on. The boys are happy that I'm home to help them with their lines. Tommy has fluffed his lines a few times, but he's so oblivious to it that we all end up laughing.

Week Ninety-one

Last week of rehearsals and everyone's mastered their parts, including Tommy. We've managed to get all their costumes online, and thankfully, from the same seller, so I paid for one postage and packaging. Tony is going to be the innkeeper; Toby, one of the shepherds, and my Tommy will be an angel.

Week Ninety-two

We are all seated in the church waiting for the play to start, and Destiny is very alert, looking around the hall. It's as if she knows her brothers are having a presentation and she doesn't want to miss a single bit of it.

* * *

It's a wonderful evening, and after the presentation, the vicar does a short sermon on Christmas followed by an altar call. I look up to see my little angel walking over to the altar. My Tommy is giving his life to Jesus. I nudge Cliff, who is equally speechless and gives me a big hug. We offer a quick prayer of thanksgiving to the Lord. Our youngest two are now saved, so it's just Tony, our eldest son, left, but Cliff and I decide not say anything to him after the show. We'll continue to pray for his salvation.

Week Ninety-three

I'm attending a women's conference in the capital and arrive during praise and worship. The lights have been dimmed, and everyone is deep in worship. The ushers wave me quickly to a lone seat a few metres away. I weave in and out of the crowd as carefully as I can so as not to disturb anyone. Half way through the praise and worship I decide to open my eyes, and whom should I see sitting next to me, Desiree Shinnay. I take a second look. It really is Desiree. I want to move seats. For some reason, Desiree decides to open her eyes, too and she seems really excited to see me, but I'm not. I'm wondering what she's doing here. Then I remember that if she's here, she's probably met the Lord, and if she hasn't, I shouldn't be a stumbling block. I keep glancing at her throughout the meeting just to see what she is up to. And then we have a tea break. I'm just about to escape when Desiree pulls me back, and with tears in her eyes, apologizes for the way she'd bullied me all through school; then she tells me she's given her heart to the Lord. Her testimony is amazing. Even her tone is different. I'm amazed. No one is beyond the reach of God's mercy. I accept Desiree's apology and then we hug, but I'm thankful for everything I went through. Desiree's constant criticism was one of those things that made me pursue my goals with tenacity. I enjoy every minute of the conference and even make new friends and get a few contacts too. Amazing! I leave the meeting with a lot of fire in my bones. I need to ignite others before it all dies down.

Week Ninety-four

I haven't had a new pair of shoes in months, but at least I get to spend time with my kids. But truth be said, I do miss being able to hit the shops. But it's only for a while. I'm investing in my kids now, and I'm sure I'll reap the benefits later.

* * *

It's my birthday today, and Cliff hasn't said anything. Not even a card. I'm shocked and sulk all through the morning, only for the postman to arrive with a package for me. I open it hurriedly and inside are the very pair of shoes I'd wanted to buy months ago, with matching accessories, from Cliff. I run up to our bedroom and Cliff is pretending to be asleep. I give him a big hug, and I tell him the story about the shoes. He laughs for several minutes, and then reminds me how much God cares about me to have him buy me the very shoes I wanted.

Week Ninety-five

Christmas is just a week to go. I take the boys shopping for a few gifts for friends and family, and an extra special one for Dora's twin girls. I'm so delighted that Dora and George aren't spending Christmas alone this year.

Week Ninety-six

It's Destiny's first Christmas, and she looks adorable in her twin set. Take lots of photos of her in different poses. She's a natural. The boys come running down to check their presents, and everyone seems happy with what they've got. Also got a "Thank you" letter from our chosen Children's Charity with photographs of the children with their Christmas presents. The boys are really thrilled that they've made other children happy. We read from the scriptures about the birth of Jesus and its significance after which we have breakfast. I've deliberately left my present unopened. Cliff has played a trick on me for the last three Christmases, leaving me an empty box under the tree only for my gift to make an appearance later, but it's always been worth the wait. He asks me why I haven't opened my gift, but I don't answer, so he brings the box to me and asks me to open it and I do. I almost choke with joy. It's a replica of my engagement ring. The original was stolen in a hotel some years ago when we'd gone on a holiday and Cliff had told me he couldn't afford to replace it, so I gave up. I hug Cliff. It's like getting engaged again, as he slips the ring onto my finger. And with our wedding anniversary just a couple of days away, it couldn't have come at a better time.

Suddenly, little white flakes begin appearing on the window sill. It's snowing. The boys jump up in excitement. We are having a white Christmas, after all. Cliff gets the logs out, and we all sit around the fireplace and sing Christmas songs as we proclaim the lordship of our Lord Jesus Christ, the Son of the living God.

Merry Christmas everyone!

www.ingramcontent.com/pod-product-compliance
Lightning Source LLC
Chambersburg PA
CBHW050911120626
46552CB00004B/1520